W9-CNO-630

No Biting, Louise

By Margie Palatini

Illustrated by

Matthew Reinhart

KATHERINE TEGEN BOOKS
An Imprint of HarperCollinsPublishers

Manufactured in China.
All rights reserved. No part of this book may be used or reproduced in any manner
whatsoever without written permission except in the case of brief quotations embodied in
critical articles and reviews. For information address HarperCollins Children's Books,
a division of HarperCollins Publishers, 1350 Avenue of the Americas, New York, NY 10019.
www.harpercollinschildrens.com

Library of Congress Cataloging-in-Publication Data
Palatini, Margie.
    No biting, Louise / by Margie Palatini; illustrated by Matthew Reinhart. — 1st ed.
        p.   cm.
    Summary: At the urging of her family, Louise, a young alligator, tries hard to kick her biting habit.
    ISBN-13: 978-0-06-052627-6 (trade bdg.) — ISBN-10: 0-06-052627-0 (trade bdg.)
    ISBN-13: 978-0-06-052628-3 (lib. bdg.) — ISBN-10: 0-06-052628-9 (lib. bdg.)
    1. Alligators—Fiction. 2. Teeth—Fiction. I. Reinhart, Matthew, ill. II. Title.
PZ7.P1755Nob 2007   2006029389
[E]—dc22

Typography by Carla Weise
1 2 3 4 5 6 7 8 9 10
❖
First Edition

For my dear friend Louise

—M.P.

To my sister, Erin,

who *is* Louise

—M.R.

Louise was a delight.

A darling.

An absolute dear.

Most of the time.

However,

upon occasion . . .

she could be just a tad . . .

trying.

Yes. There was that tendency to . . .

how to put it?

Gnaw?

On everything. Everyone. Everywhere.

Louise promised Mother:
Absolutely no more biting.
Nope.
Never.
Ever.

Louise fibbed.

"Ouch!"

Mother was not pleased with Louise.

Louise was sorry.

She was really, really, truly quite sorry.

It was just that she
was so proud of her new
gleaming-white baby
choppers.

Try as she might—
and she tried,
she truly tried—

Louise could not resist the temptation to nibble.

Louise meant no harm in a chomp or two
now and then. Surely everyone knew that.

They did not.

Except—for Grandmama Sadie.

"Nana's little love," she cooed and hugged.
"Tsk. Tsk. Tsk. Such bother over a little biting.
A few nibbles. A smattering of some carefree
chomps. Such pooh!"

"Not to worry," said Grandmama. "I am quite
sure, totally positive, mark my words, that this
is only a phase my little joy is going through.
She will outgrow it!"

"And hopefully . . .

Soon."

And . . . she did!

Thankfully. Most gratefully. Louise did indeed.

Just as Grandmama Sadie predicted, all in good time there was no more biting from Louise.

The problem now—

was something else entirely.

BURP.

BURP.

BURP.

"Chew, Louise, chew," instructed Mother. "My dear, you must remember to chew everything well before you swallow."

BURP.

Louise was going to
have to work on that.